Pickles

and the
P-Flock Bullies

Written by **Stephen Cosgrove**
Illustrated by **Robin James**

little bigfoot

an imprint of sasquatch books
seattle, wa

Manufactured in China by C&C Offset Printing Co. Ltd. Shanghai,
in January 2014

Published by Little Bigfoot, an imprint of Sasquatch Books
18 17 16 15 14   9 8 7 6 5 4 3 2 1

Editor: Christy Cox
Project editor: Michelle Hope Anderson
Illustrations: Robin James
Design: Anna Goldstein

Library of Congress Cataloging-in-Publication Data is available.

ISBN: 978-1-57061-887-1

Sasquatch Books
1904 Third Avenue, Suite 710
Seattle, WA 98101
(206) 467-4300
www.sasquatchbooks.com
custserv@sasquatchbooks.com

Dedicated to my favorite frolicking flock:
Gage, Hunter, and Jessie Rae (which is
spelled every which way but right).
Grand and good children deserving
of a dedication such as this.

—Stephen/Grm'Pa

There is a place, a magical place of sparkling waters and whispering winds. There are few words that can truly express its beauty, for like a billowing silk scarf these waters embrace all that lies between the majestic Olympic Mountains and the Emerald City of Seattle. They call this place the Puget Sound.

But this is more than a place of magical metaphor; it is a body of water that teems with ever-changing life, from fish to fowl, from man to mammal.

Of the mammals that live here, none is more majestic than the mighty Orca, the killer whale. With fins like blackened sails, pods of Orca glide through the inky waters of the Sound.

Here they hunt.

Here they play.

Here they live their lives away.

Wondrous things happen in the waters here, but none quite as unique as the birth of a very special Orca calf.

Normally Orcas are born with bright white patches behind their eyes, behind their fins, and yet another along their belly. But what made this newborn so unique was that some of her patches were not white, nor even faded gray. They were as green as the evergreen trees that border the rocky beaches of the mighty Sound.

Her birth name was Tickles, but all of the whales in her pod delightfully called her Pickles.

Save for the green patches, Pickles was as perfect as perfect could be. Normal that is—like you and me.

Unfortunately, being the only child in the pod left Pickles with no one to play with.

O ne day as Pickles swam alone near the pebbled shore, she happened upon a harbor seal basking on the beach. She moved closer and closer until the smooth rocks scraped her belly.

"Hello!" she said brightly.

The harbor seal looked back at her, his eyes widened with fear, and he began frantically flopping toward the open water.

"Where are you going?" Pickles asked.

"Anywhere but here!" squealed the seal.

"But why?"

The harbor seal twisted around and exposed his backside that was laced with a spiderweb of scars.

"Why? Because the last time I saw an Orca I almost became a mammal meal. Now everyone calls me Stitches!"

"Well," huffed Pickles, "I would never eat you. I am just looking for someone to play with."

And so it was that Stitches and Pickles became fast friends.

The next several days were filled with gurgles and giggles as they frolicked in the Sound playing watery games of tickle tag and dunk and dive.

It was a rough-and-tumble kind of play, but without an ounce of meanness or malice.

Every evening as the sun settled beyond the majestic Olympic Mountains, they would watch the feathery clouds turn from pink to purple to deep night-sky blue.

One day the two friends surfaced in the still waters of a place called Bitter Berry Bay. Years gone by, the bay had been a bustling timber mill, but now the only thing that remained was an old moss-covered wharf, long beyond repair. The barnacled pilings were wrapped in bitter berry vines, the purple fruit rotting and very sour.

Strutting on the wharf was an unusual flock of seagulls. Their beaks were bright yellow with a red berry-like button at the bottom, and their wings were tipped with a bit of blue. But most unusual were the long downy feathers that graced their heads. They stood, some on one leg, some on two, preening each other, styling their head feathers in the most adventurous of ways.

As they preened they noticed the whale and the seal bobbing in the bay. One of them waddled to the end of the wharf and said, "Aha! What do we have here?"

"My name is Pickles and this is Stitches," the little Orca said shyly. "We are looking for new friends."

W ell," the seagull clucked, "specific friends or will anyone do?"

The other gulls stomped their webbed feet, chuckling in delight at this bit of witticism.

"Anyone will do," laughed Pickles.

"Well then, let me introduce us. We are the P Flock. *P* stands for pretty, for simply spoken we are very, very pretty. My name is Pomp," he said. He stretched his wing in a modest bow, pointing at the rest of the flock. "The others are Precious, Princess, Privy, Plume, and Priss, and way too many others to list."

He smiled a beaky little smile that seagulls are wont to do and announced, "Little whale, you can join us because you are very pretty too!"

Pickles quickly accepted their offer of friendship.

As Pickles was greeted with the delighted cackles and caws of the P Flock on the wharf, Stitches called out brightly, "Me too? Can I be a member too?"

Pomp smiled a sticky sweet smile and sniped in a singsong voice, "Stitches! Stitches! Stitches! There may be a little bitty problem with you and the P Flock."

Stitches blinked his big, brown eyes. "Problem? What problem?"

Pomp waddled closer to Stitches and whispered loudly, "You see, little seal, it's all about being pretty. And as you know, you are not very pretty, what with the scars and all. So it would be best if you left Bitter Berry Bay and found others of your kind."

"I'm not going anywhere," the seal said defiantly. "I will stay here with my friend Pickles. I can be here if I want to!"

O h, dear. This will never do!" snickered Pomp. "Bitter Berry Bay is private, for the P Flock only! No scarred harbor seals allowed, ever!"

His webbed feet flapping on the weathered wood wharf, he moved quickly to the vine-draped pilings. Using his beak, he plucked a rotting berry from the vine. Then, flapping his wings, he ran the length of the wharf and lifted into the air.

In a flutter of wings, the rest of the flock plucked overripe berries from the brambles and followed.

Screeching loudly, they swooped down, dropping the berries on the seal's head. The juice of the rotten berries bitterly burned the little seal's eyes.

Pickles was now an official member of the P Flock, and so, without thinking, she joined in the bullying. Laughing, she breached high into the air and dropped heavily back into the bay, splashing Stitches in a mighty wave of water.

Sputtering, Stitches cried out, "Pickles, why are you doing this to me? What have I done to you? I thought we were friends!"

Pickles didn't really know how to answer. She just floated there, her big eyes blinking, not feeling very happy about what she had just done.

Pomp laughed as he circled overhead. "You dumb seal, Pickles is a P!"

The harbor seal, with a tear in his eye, slowly swam from the bay, his berry-splattered head laying low in the water.

Pickles turned to her new friends and softly said, "Maybe we shouldn't have been so mean."

With wings cupped, Pomp glided back down to the wharf and began chattering quietly to Priss. Pickles couldn't understand what they were saying over the staccato clacking of their bills. Suddenly the birds burst into a fit of laughter.

Smiling, she swam a bit closer. "What are you gulls laughing at?"

"Oh, it's nothing you would be interested in, little whale," Pomp snickered.

"Yeah, nothing a whale like you would even understand," added Priss.

Pomp winked at his fellow feathered P-Flock members and led them to the other end of the wharf.

For a while the gulls of the P Flock gossiped, their beaks clicking like hard leather shoes on a sidewalk. "She is definitely green," giggled Priss, "but maybe Pickles isn't a big enough word for her."

"Yeah," sneered Pomp, "maybe they should have called her Watermelon." And they all laughed and laughed.

All the while Pickles floated quietly in the water, unable to make out what they were laughing about. Finally, she took a deep breath and swam closer.

"Shh!" the gulls giggled. "Here she comes!"

"What are you laughing about?" Pickles asked.

Pomp smiled sweetly, "Oh, nothing, nothing at all—just a little whale joke."

"Or," snickered Priss, "a big, fat whale joke as your case may be."

It was then Pickles realized that she was the whale joke.

Saddened, with large oily tears welling in her eyes, Pickles slowly swam from Bitter Berry Bay, the sound of the gulls' vicious laughter echoing in her ears.

It was one thing to be a bully, but quite another to be bullied. She swam sadly into the openness of Puget Sound.

As a full moon rose over the Sound, she found herself bathed in the colorful lights of nighttime Seattle dancing on the waves.

Here, she also found Stitches the harbor seal bobbing in the water. Silently they watched the cityscape without speaking. Each time a wave moved them closer together, the seal pushed away. Finally Pickles sighed. "I am so sorry that I was a bully," she whispered.

Stitches said nothing, but the next time a wave moved them closer together, he didn't move away.

So it was that Pickles and Stitches renewed their friendship, vowing to never be the bully or be bullied again.

If you find yourself being bullied

Or if a bully you would rather be,

Remember this story of Pickles

And all that she came to see.